Our Family Band

written by Pam Holden
illustrated by Robin Van't Hof

1

Our family loves music.
My mother likes to play
her violin.

It goes like this:
vvvVVVvvv vvvVVVvvv

My father plays the music
he likes on his guitar.

Listen to this: strum-strum

My brother plays the music
he likes on his trumpet.

It goes like this:
oompa-oompa oompa-oompa

My sister plays the music
she loves on her ukelele.

She goes like this:
strum-strum-strum

My grandfather plays
the music he likes on
his bagpipes.

They go like this:
ppprrumm-pprrumm-pprrumm

My grandmother plays the music she loves on her piano.

Listen to this: la la la la

I play the music I like
on my drums.

They go like this:
rat-a-tat tat **tat tat!**

Our dog loves music too!
He likes to sing like this:
Ooooo OOO oooo OOO!